Abby and the Book Bunch

OUT TO LUNCH

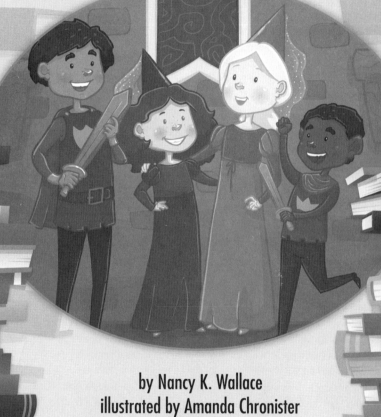

by Nancy K. Wallace
illustrated by Amanda Chronister

magic
wagon

visit us at www.abdopublishing.com

For my husband, Dennie, and my original Book Bunch: Hanna, Derrick, & Dakota
—NW

Published by Magic Wagon, a division of the ABDO Group, PO Box 398166, Minneapolis, MN 55439. Copyright © 2013 by Abdo Consulting Group, Inc. International copyrights reserved in all countries. All rights reserved. No part of this book may be reproduced in any form without written permission from the publisher.

Calico Chapter Books™ is a trademark and logo of Magic Wagon.

Printed in the United States of America, North Mankato, Minnesota.
102012
012013
This book contains at least 10% recycled materials.

Text by Nancy K. Wallace
Illustrations by Amanda Chronister
Edited by Stephanie Hedlund and Rochelle Baltzer
Layout and design by Neil Klinepier

Library of Congress Cataloging-in-Publication Data
Wallace, Nancy K.
  Out to lunch / by Nancy K. Wallace ; illustrated by Amanda Chronister.
    p. cm. -- (Abby and the Book Bunch)
  Summary: Between working on the medieval project for third grade and helping move books and redecorate the children's section at the public library, Abby Spencer and her friends, the Book Bunch, have their hands full--but Mrs. Mackenzie has promised them a really special lunch as a reward.
  ISBN 978-1-61641-916-5
  1. Public libraries--Juvenile fiction. 2. Volunteers--Juvenile fiction. 3. Books and reading--Juvenile fiction. 4. Elementary schools--Juvenile fiction. [1. Public libraries--Fiction. 2. Voluntarism--Fiction. 3. Books and reading--Fiction. 4. Elementary schools--Fiction. 5. Schools--Fiction.] I. Chronister, Amanda, ill. II. Title.
  PZ7.W158752Out 2013
  813.54--dc23
                                    2012029483

Sydney laughed. "Snow and cold go together! Whoever heard of warm snow?"

They stamped the snow off of their boots at the library's front door.

"I hope the library is warm," Abby said. "I think we're going to be busy today. Mrs. Mackenzie said she had a lot for us to do."

Mrs. Mackenzie was the children's librarian. Abby and her friends liked helping out at the library after school. After a school community service project ended, they continued helping there. Mrs. Mackenzie called them Abby and the Book Bunch! She always found fun jobs for them to do.

"When we're done helping Mrs. Mackenzie, we can work on our medieval project," Sydney said. "We need to decide on a subject."

"Hi, girls!" Mrs. Mackenzie's voice came from up above them.

Abby and Sydney looked up. Mrs. Mackenzie was standing on a ladder. Red hearts covered with glitter dangled from the ceiling. They hung by paperclips all over the ladder, too.

Mrs. Mackenzie smiled. "I'm glad you are here! I really need your help today. I still have 100 hearts to hang!"

Sydney groaned. "One hundred more?" she asked.

Mrs. Mackenzie laughed. "I'm just kidding. I think there are only about two dozen left." She climbed down the ladder. "Why don't you put your coats in my office?"

Abby and Sydney followed Mrs. Mackenzie. Glitter sparkled in her hair and on her clothes. It drifted around her like tiny snowflakes. She left a sparkly trail across the library as she walked.

Abby giggled. "Poor Art and Lois," she whispered to Sydney. She felt sorry for the custodians. There was always glitter on the floor of Mrs. Mackenzie's office. Glitter covered most of the library carpet today, too!

They hung up their coats in Mrs. Mackenzie's office. Abby stashed their book bags under the desk. She was careful not to bump anything.

Abby turned around. Mrs. Mackenzie stood at the door. She had her hands folded in front her. Her eyes twinkled. "I have a surprise!" she said.

"For us?" Abby asked.

"For all the kids!" said Mrs. Mackenzie. She gave an excited little hop. "An anonymous donor gave some money to the Children's Area!"

Abby frowned. "What does anonymous mean?" she asked.

"It means the person doesn't want us to tell his or her name," Mrs. Mackenzie said. "He gave us a gift, but he doesn't want anyone to know who did it."

Abby shook her head. "Why would anyone do that?"

Mrs. Mackenzie shrugged. "Some people do nice things to make other people happy. They just don't want anyone to make a fuss about it."

"Is it a lot of money?" Sydney asked.

"There is enough for some new bookcases and books. There will be enough left over to buy new toys, too!" Mrs. Mackenzie said.

"Wow," said Abby.

"I'm ordering some shelves to go along the wall by the window," Mrs. Mackenzie said. "When the bookcases are delivered, a lot of books will have to be moved. I'm going to need some help!"

"We'll help!" Abby and Sydney said together.

Mrs. Mackenzie smiled. "I was sure I could count on the Book Bunch. Thank you!"

"We'll make sure Dakota and Zachary help, too!" Abby said.

Sydney looked at Mrs. Mackenzie's desk. "What's all this paint for?"

Mrs. Mackenzie couldn't stop smiling. "That's part of the project, too. We want the children's department to look special. I've gotten permission to paint some murals on the walls!"

"Sweet!" said Sydney.

"You girls spend so much time in the library," Mrs. Mackenzie said, "I'd like you to help me choose what kinds of pictures to paint."

Abby clapped her hands. "This will be so much fun!"

"I want to thank all of you for helping me," Mrs. Mackenzie said. "I'm going to take the Book Bunch out to lunch when this project is over!"

"Where are we going?" Sydney asked.

Mrs. Mackenzie's eyes twinkled. "I haven't decided yet," she said. "But it will be some place very special!"

Abby and Sydney looked at each other. They could hardly wait!

Project Problems

Abby perched on the library ladder. She hooked the last sparkly red heart onto a ceiling tile and climbed down. "Can you help me take this ladder back?" she asked Sydney.

"Sure," said Sydney. They pushed the ladder back to the stacks together.

"I wonder who he is," Abby said as they passed the reading area.

Sydney looked at the people reading books, magazines, and newspapers. "Who are you talking about?" she asked.

"The man who gave the money to the children's department," Abby whispered.

Sydney turned to look all around the library. "What makes you think he's here?"

Abby shrugged. "Mrs. Mackenzie didn't mention the money when we were here yesterday. So, it must have come today."

"Or she could have waited until today to tell us," Sydney suggested. "Maybe the money came in the mail."

"Maybe," Abby said. "But I think that whoever gave money to the library must use the library a lot. I'll bet we have seen him in here." She looked closely at the people on the chairs and couch.

Sydney pointed. "There's that newspaper reporter. Maybe he gave money to the library."

Abby shook her head. "I don't think so. He doesn't have any kids."

"The person doesn't have to have kids," Sydney protested.

"I'll bet he has kids," Abby said. "Why would someone give money to the children's department if he didn't have kids?"

"I don't know," Sydney said.

Abby saw a familiar face. She waved at her neighbor, Mr. Jackson.

"Mr. Jackson has two little girls and he's a writer," she whispered when Mr. Jackson waved back. "He probably loves libraries!"

Sydney nodded. "I bet he's the one!"

Abby frowned. "But maybe he didn't do it," she added. "He just moved here. He hasn't been coming to our library very long."

"Maybe it isn't a man," Sydney said. "Did you think of that?"

Suddenly, Mrs. Mackenzie appeared between the bookshelves. A shimmering cloud of glitter followed behind her.

"How does she do that?" Sydney whispered. "Doesn't all the glitter ever fall off?"

Abby shook her head and looked at the floor. She almost expected to see glitter falling off her own shoulders.

Mrs. Mackenzie smiled. "Thank you for putting the ladder back!" she said.

"Do you have time to put a few books away?"

"Sure," said Abby.

They followed Mrs. Mackenzie to the Children's Area. Mrs. Mackenzie shimmered and twinkled with every step!

"Can you help us find some books for our project?" Abby asked.

"We need to get started. We have to tell Mr. Kim what we will be doing on Friday," Sydney said. "Then we have two weeks to finish our projects."

"What are you studying?" Mrs. Mackenzie asked.

"Medieval times," Abby answered. "Everyone has to make a project and then show it to the class. Sydney and I want to work together on something."

Mrs. Mackenzie frowned. "The subject is medieval times? I checked out a lot of medieval books yesterday to Miss Pringle's students. I didn't realize both classes were doing projects on the same subject."

Abby nodded. "Both third grade classes are studying medieval times. Mr. Kim's class and Miss Pringle's class are having a contest. Whichever class has the best projects wins a pizza party! We weren't supposed to start until today."

"Oh dear," said Mrs. Mackenzie. "I'd better reserve some books for library use only. Otherwise there won't be enough books for everyone!"

Abby looked at Sydney. "What if the other class already checked out all the medieval books?" Abby asked.

Abby, Sydney, and Mrs. Mackenzie rushed to look. The shelf was empty!

"What will we do now?" Abby wailed.

The Restricted Section

"Don't panic," Mrs. Mackenzie said. "I still have books that you can use."

"But all the medieval books are gone!" Sydney said. "We're not allowed to do our reports on anything else!"

"I still have medieval books," Mrs. Mackenzie explained. "The library has books called reference books. They can't be checked out, but you can use them here at the library. I have reference books on all kinds of subjects."

"Where are they?" Abby asked.

"They're behind the circulation desk in the restricted section. You just have to request the books from a librarian," said Mrs. Mackenzie.

Sydney's eyes grew big. "The restricted section?" she asked. "That's just like the library in the Harry Potter books!"

Mrs. Mackenzie laughed. "Well, most libraries have a restricted section," she said. "Some libraries may not call it that. But all libraries have books that can't go out of the building."

"Why?" asked Abby. "Don't they want people to use them?"

Mrs. Mackenzie shook her head. "We *do* want people to use them. But there are times when all the books on a subject are checked out. Just like today! Then we are lucky we still have reference books to use."

"We really are lucky!" Abby said. "Or we wouldn't be able to do our project."

Mrs. Mackenzie walked toward the circulation desk. "Come with me," she said. "I'll show you where the reference books are."

Abby had seen the restricted section before. But she hadn't paid much attention to it. The books were shelved in bookcases that reached clear to the ceiling. The staff used long ladders to reach them.

"Aren't these books just for adults?" Abby asked.

Mrs. Mackenzie nodded. "A lot of them are. But there are children's books, too."

Abby touched two fat, brown books. The covers were cracked and old. The titles were so worn she couldn't read them.

"What are these books?" she asked.

"Those are local history books," Mrs. Mackenzie said. "They are very old and rare. If something happened to them they couldn't be replaced. That's why they are in the restricted section."

Mrs. Mackenzie climbed up three steps on the ladder. She chose five books with bright blue covers off the shelf. "Take a look at these," she said, climbing down.

Abby took the books to a table. She looked at each one carefully. The first book showed a huge castle. Two knights raced their horses toward each other on the cover of the second book. The third book showed a medieval town.

"Oh, look!" Abby said when she saw the fourth book. It showed ladies in long velvet dresses on the front. They had tall, cone-shaped hats on their heads.

"Those dresses are so pretty!" Sydney said. "Maybe we could dress up like those ladies!"

Abby turned to look at her and grinned. "That would be so much fun!"

Mrs. Mackenzie laughed. "Oh dear, it sounds like Gram is going to be doing some sewing."

"Gram really loves to sew!" Abby said. "And Sydney and I will help her."

"I bet we can make those hats ourselves," Sydney said. "Then we'll look like princesses."

"I'd love to look like a princess!" Abby said.

Sydney bounced up and down. "This is going to be a great project!" she said.

Abby glanced at Sydney. "We can't just dress up," she reminded her. "We have to write a report, too."

Mrs. Mackenzie picked up one of the books. "Maybe you could find some information about real princesses," she said. "You could write your report about them. Then you can dress up when you give your report to the class."

"That's a great idea!" Abby said. "Will you help us?"

"Of course," said Mrs. Mackenzie. "Let's sit down and look at these books. I'm sure we'll find lots of things you can use."

Abby and Sydney spun around in a little happy dance! Then they sat down in chairs next to Mrs. Mackenzie. This project was going to be a lot of fun! And maybe their class would win the pizza party, too!

Knights of the Lunch Table

Crack! Crack! Snap! Half a pretzel stick flew across the lunch table.

"Look out!" Dakota yelled, jumping back.

The pretzel chunk crashed onto Sydney's lunch tray. Applesauce splattered all over Sydney's white shirt. It dripped off Abby's hair and onto her face.

"Dakota!" Abby gasped.

Sydney jumped up. She glared at Dakota and Zachary. "That's it!" she said. "No more sword fights with food!"

Abby blinked applesauce out of her eye. She wiped her face with a napkin.

"Yesterday, you fought with carrot sticks and you spilled my milk!" she said. "Today you are dueling with pretzels!"

Sydney put her hands on her hips. "Stop it or we'll tell Mr. Kim!"

Dakota clutched two pretzel sticks in his hand. "We were just practicing," he protested.

"Don't practice at lunch!" Sydney said. She scrubbed at her shirt with her napkin.

"We want to be like the Knights of the Round Table!" Zachary said proudly.

Abby giggled. "Well, right now you're only the knights of the lunch table!"

"Yeah," said Sydney. "Instead of brave and courageous, you're just annoying."

Zachary gestured with a pretzel stick. "Well, we can't help it if we don't have real swords!"

"Why don't you practice with sticks in your yard?" Abby grumbled. "Just stop throwing food at lunch. Our table is always the messiest one!"

Sydney stared at the spot on her shirt. She nudged Abby. "Does applesauce stain?" she asked. "This is a new shirt."

"I don't know," Abby replied. "But I'm sure Dakota's mom will buy you a new one if it does."

"Don't tell my mom!" Dakota protested.

"Then don't throw food!" Sydney said.

"You girls are no fun at all," Dakota said.

Abby tapped her fingers on the table. She was thinking about all the time Mrs. Mackenzie had spent helping them find books for their project. "What if you had real swords?" she asked. "That would make a great project!"

Zachary's mouth dropped open. "Where would we find real swords?"

"Well, they wouldn't be real exactly," Abby said. "But Mrs. Mackenzie has pictures of what medieval swords looked like. What if Sydney and I helped you make swords out of cardboard?"

"We already tried that," Dakota said. "They bend when we hit them together."

"What if they were made of wood?" Abby asked.

Zachary nodded excitedly. "Wooden swords would be good!" he said.

"Where are you going to get wooden swords?" Dakota asked.

"My dad has a workshop out in the garage," Abby said. "He cuts out stuff for my mom all the time. I'll bet he would make swords for you."

"Wow!" Dakota said.

"Let's go to the library tomorrow and copy a picture of a sword," said Abby. "If you can draw two swords, I'm sure he will cut them out for you. You can paint them for your project."

"This will be so cool!" Dakota said.

Abby ran a hand cautiously through her hair. "Just don't throw any more pretzels," she said.

"Or spill any more milk or applesauce," Sydney added.

"Don't worry. We won't!" said Dakota.

Zachary slapped Dakota's hand. "This is going to be awesome!" he said.

Swords and Shields

"It's freezing out here!" Sydney complained. She huddled near the electric heater in Abby's garage. "You owe us big time, Dakota!"

"I know. I know," Dakota said. He had his arms folded over his chest. His blue mittens were tucked under his arms. "But look how awesome these swords are going to be!"

Abby grinned. Dakota's cheeks glowed bright red in the cold garage. His eyes sparkled. She could tell how excited he was.

Abby's dad blew sawdust off the plywood. "I'm almost done," he said. "I want to make sure this handle comes out just right."

"It's called the hilt," Dakota told him. "I read about the parts of the sword for my report."

Abby's dad nodded. "I think I've heard that term before. It sounds like you are learning a lot from this project."

"Mrs. Mackenzie found some really great books," Abby said. "She has spent so much time helping us with our projects."

Dakota frowned. "She had to help us because Miss Pringle's class checked out all the books first," he added grimly.

Abby's dad smiled. "Mrs. Mackenzie is a nice lady. We're lucky to have such a great librarian in town."

Abby rubbed her hands together. "We still don't know where Mrs. Mackenzie is taking us to lunch," she said. "She says it's a surprise."

Zachary stamped his feet and jogged in place. His face was buried in his woolly scarf. "Maybe we're going to Pizza Jack's," he suggested.

Abby shook her head. "Mrs. Mackenzie said she was taking us somewhere really special."

"Maybe we're going to that restaurant downtown," said Sydney. "It's called the Zen Garden. It has a stream that runs through the dining room."

Zachary looked up. "Do they have cheeseburgers?" he asked hopefully.

"I don't think so," Sydney said. "They serve Chinese food."

"Oh man," Zachary complained.

The saw buzzed one last time. A piece of wood dropped with a bang onto the floor. "That's it!" announced Mr. Spencer. "I'm done!"

"Thanks for helping, Mr. Spencer," Dakota said. "My dad doesn't have a saw."

Abby's dad took off his safety glasses. "I don't mind at all. I like doing this sort of thing." He held up a sword in each hand. "There you go, boys!"

Dakota grabbed a sword. He jabbed it at Zachary.

Zachary jumped to one side. He smacked Dakota's sword with his. "Surrender!" cried Zachary.

"Never!" yelled Dakota, scooting backward. He fell over a stack of plastic flowerpots and landed on his back.

Zachary held his sword to Dakota's throat. "Surrender or die!" he growled.

"Hold it!" Abby's dad warned them. "No fighting inside the garage! Put your swords down for a minute. I have a little surprise for you."

Zachary grabbed Dakota's hand and pulled him up. They held their swords at their sides.

Abby's dad picked up a cloth sack from the table. "Abby told me about the contest between the two third grade classes," he said. "I thought maybe this might help your class win."

Dakota danced with excitement. "What did you make?" he asked.

"I had some wood left over from another project. I made each of you a shield, too," said Abby's dad. "You'll have to paint them. Maybe you can make up your own coat of arms."

Zachary frowned. "What's a coat of arms?" he asked.

"During medieval times, important families put symbols on their shields," Abby's dad said. "I'm sure Mrs. Mackenzie can find you some pictures of them." He handed Zachary and Dakota their shields.

"Wow! Thanks!" Dakota said. "Ours is going to be the best project of all!"

"No way!" protested Sydney. "Being a princess is way cooler than being a knight!"

Abby's dad laughed. "I think all of you are going to have great projects. Too bad you'll only get to use your costumes one time."

"We can wear them again for Halloween," Abby suggested.

"That's months away!" Sydney protested.

"I'm sure you'll think of something," Abby's dad said. "Come on. Mom has hot cocoa and cookies for all of you. Let's go in before we freeze!"

Dakota and Zachary leaped out of the garage door. They spun and jumped with their swords. Puffs of snow flew through the air as they attacked every tree and bush in the yard.

Abby laughed. She and Sydney ran into the house. Hot cocoa sounded so good!

Marvelous Murals!

Abby ran into the library Monday after school. She raced to the children's area and zipped around two toddlers playing with blocks on the rug. Mrs. Mackenzie was putting books away.

"Mrs. Mackenzie!" Abby gasped. "I have an awesome idea!"

Mrs. Mackenzie turned around with a stack of books in her arms. "An idea about what?" she asked.

Abby took a deep breath. "You know how you said you were going to paint murals on the walls?"

Mrs. Mackenzie nodded.

"Why don't you paint castles and knights and princesses?" Abby asked.

"You could paint a dragon, too!"

"That's a very good idea!" Mrs. Mackenzie said with a smile. "When did you think of that?"

Abby set her book bag down on the floor. "I thought of it at school today," she replied. "You copied all those medieval pictures for me. We were looking at them at lunchtime. Castles would make the children's area look like part of a fairy tale!"

Mrs. Mackenzie turned slowly in a circle. She looked at the beige walls around her. "I think you are right!" she said. "That is an awesome idea!"

Abby looked at the two bookcases that formed the entrance to the Children's Area. "Would you be allowed to paint these bookcases?" she asked.

Mrs. Mackenzie made a face. "I don't know. I'm not sure the library director would like that idea. Those bookcases are oak. What color were you thinking of painting them?"

"Could you paint them to look like stones?" Abby asked. "I was thinking that we could make them look like an arch. Then it would feel as though you were walking into a real castle!"

Mrs. Mackenzie walked around the toddlers. She looked at the other side of the bookcases.

"We'll have to think about this," Mrs. Mackenzie said. "Maybe we wouldn't have to paint the bookcases. Maybe someone could make us a wooden arch that fits over them. Then I could just paint the arch!"

"My dad could do that!" Abby offered.

Mrs. Mackenzie laughed. "Your father has already done so much! Didn't he just make swords and shields for Zachary and Dakota? We don't want to wear him out!"

Abby shook her head. "He really likes to do things like that! Can I ask him?"

Mrs. Mackenzie nodded. "I guess it would be okay," she said. "Go ahead and ask him. I think this is a very good idea. What else do you think I should paint over here?"

Abby ran to the window seat. It was covered with books and toys. "You could

paint stones around the windows, too," she said. "It would look like you were inside the castle!"

Mrs. Mackenzie smiled. "And where should the dragon go?" she asked. "Is he allowed to be inside the castle, too?"

Abby shook her head. "No, I think he should stay outside." She pointed to the wall on the other side of the bookcases. "Maybe he could be flying toward the castle."

"That would work," said Mrs. Mackenzie. "I think I would like to paint a gold dragon with glittery wings."

Abby held out her arms. "He should be really big and really tall."

"And he could be flying over a little village," Mrs. Mackenzie added. "It looks like I need to get busy and make some sketches."

Abby touched the blank wall beside her. "You could paint some princesses right here," she said.

Mrs. Mackenzie put her hands on her hips. "Now let's see," she said. "Can you think of anywhere I could get models to pose for the princesses?"

"Sydney and I would do it!" Abby said, jumping up and down. "Wait until Gram finishes our dresses. We'll pose for you!"

Mrs. Mackenzie grinned. "I thought you might! Maybe Zachary and Dakota will pose as knights, too. I can have a picture of my Book Bunch right here on the library wall!"

"Forever and ever," Abby said, twirling around.

Mrs. Mackenzie clapped her hands. "Oh, Abby," she said, "I think this is a wonderful idea. I can hardly wait to start!"

Medieval Madness

Sydney went to Abby's house after school on Friday. They only had a few things left to finish for their project.

Gram greeted them at the door. She smiled and bowed low. "Good afternoon, Your Royal Highnesses," she said. "Your gowns are ready!"

Two long dresses hung in the hallway. One was purple. The other one was pink.

"Oh, Gram, they're beautiful!" Abby cried. She threw her arms around Gram and hugged her tight.

Sydney fingered the pretty pink fabric. "I love mine," she said. "Thank you so much, Mrs. Simon!"

"It was my pleasure," said Gram. "I had fun making them!"

A sad howl and the sound of scratching came from the kitchen. The girls turned to look at the closed door.

Gram laughed. "I shut Lucy in the kitchen so she wouldn't drool on your dresses."

"I'll go and see her," Abby offered. "She can drool on me."

Abby opened the door and closed it behind her. Lucy, Abby's golden retriever, jumped up and down. She wagged her tail furiously.

Abby patted her long, silky ears. "Did you miss me today?" she asked.

Lucy rubbed her head against Abby. She smiled a happy dog smile.

"It's safe to let Lucy out!" Gram called from upstairs. "I put the dresses in your bedroom and closed the door."

Abby opened the door. Lucy bounded into the hall. She greeted Sydney with her wet, sloppy kisses.

"Thanks for the kisses!" Sydney giggled. She wiped her hand on her jeans.

Gram came down the stairs. "Do you need any help with your medieval hats?"

"Yes, please," said Abby. "We have to figure out a pattern."

They took cardboard, glue, and scissors to the kitchen. Lucy lay down under the table. Her tail thumped happily on the floor.

"I found these old scarves," said Gram. "I thought you could use them on the tops of your hats."

One scarf was silver. The other one was gold.

Abby took a picture of the medieval hats from her book bag. "Those are just what we needed, Gram. Thanks!" She turned to look at Sydney. "Which one do you want?"

Sydney shrugged. "You pick first."

"I like the gold one," Abby said. She draped it around her neck and waved the end. "Don't I look charming?"

Sydney grabbed the silver one. She put it over her head and laughed. "Yes!" she said. "And so do I!"

"They are perfect for our costumes!" Abby said.

Abby used a piece of purple cardboard for her hat. Gram helped her make a pattern so the hat would fit right. Abby carefully spread glue down the seam. Sydney helped her hold it together while the glue dried.

"I sure hope we win this contest," Sydney said. "Dakota showed me his shield today. It looks great!"

Abby giggled. "Guess what, Gram?" she said. "Dakota wanted to paint a soccer ball for his coat of arms. Mrs. Mackenzie persuaded him to use a horse instead."

"It's a really nice horse," Sydney said. "He did a good job!"

"It sounds as though everyone in your class is working hard," said Gram.

"I wish we knew that everyone's project was special," Abby said. "We really want to win!"

Sydney got her notebook out of her book bag. "I did some research," she said. "Katie is making medieval food. Her mom is helping her. Her report is going to have recipes in it."

"That's a good project," said Abby. "What about Ethan?

Sydney looked at her list. "Ethan is making a banner."

"Okay," Abby said.

"And Morgan told me she's making a tapestry out of paper," Sydney added. "It has a million little pieces. I think she'll do a good job."

"Wow," said Abby. "Those are good projects!"

Sydney leaned back in her chair. "I can taste that pizza already!"

"Just do the best that you can," Gram said. "You can be proud of your project no matter what happens. You've done a lot of work for your report and your costumes are great!"

Abby groaned. "But we want to win the pizza party!"

"I'm sure the other class is working hard, too," Gram reminded her. "They probably want to win just as much as you do."

"We want to win more!" said Sydney laughing.

But Abby didn't laugh. She was sure Miss Pringle's class did want to win, too. She sighed and patted Lucy's head.

Frogs and Dragons

Abby, Sydney, and Dakota stopped at the library after school on Wednesday. Everyone in their class had finished their reports with Mrs. Mackenzie's help. The contest was only two days away! It was hard to think about anything else.

"I can hardly wait until Friday!" Dakota said. He stabbed his pencil at the bulletin board like a sword. "We're going to win! I just know it!"

"Miss Pringle's class doesn't stand a chance," Sydney replied confidently.

"I hope you're right," said Abby as they walked into the children's area.

A blue and green rug shaped like a pond covered the Story Time area.

Two giant frog pillows crouched near its edge. Four new bookcases stood against the wall.

"Wow, look at all this!" Abby said.

Dakota collapsed onto the rug. "Help, I can't swim!" he yelled. He pretended to splash in the water. "Pull me out! I'm drowning!"

Sydney rolled her eyes. "Sorry," she said, "Abby and I don't want to get our feet wet."

Mrs. Mackenzie appeared around the corner with a bag of brightly colored blocks. "Hey," she said. "There's my Book Bunch! Look at all this great stuff we got!"

"This looks really nice!" Abby said.

Sydney flopped down on a frog pillow. "I wish you'd had frog pillows when I was coming to Story Time!" she said.

Abby sat down on the other one. "They are really soft! This is a great place to read!"

"Wait until you see the dragon!" Mrs. Mackenzie said. "It's in my office."

"Do you want me to get it?" Dakota offered.

"I thought you were drowning," Sydney said.

Mrs. Mackenzie frowned and looked at Dakota. "When were you drowning?" she asked.

Abby giggled.

"Don't ask," Sydney said, rolling her eyes.

"You can get the dragon, Dakota," Mrs. Mackenzie said. "He's wrapped up in plastic. Just take it off before you bring him over here."

Dakota zipped off toward Mrs. Mackenzie's office.

"Do you need us to move some books today?" Abby asked.

"That would be wonderful if you have time," said Mrs. Mackenzie. "It's going to take us a couple of days to move them all. Some of the shelves are just packed. The new bookcases will let us spread the books out a little. Then there will be some extra room on every shelf."

"We can help tomorrow after school and on Saturday morning," Sydney said. "But Monday afternoon is the pizza party. We won't be able to help that day!"

Mrs. Mackenzie looked a little worried. "Well, just in case the pizza party doesn't work out," she said, "don't forget that I'm taking you out to lunch, too."

Dakota arrived dragging a huge stuffed dragon. It had gold horns and a long, spiky tail. It was big enough for a toddler to ride on!

"This is so cute!" Abby said, touching its beautiful horns.

"I hope the kids won't fight over him," Mrs. Mackenzie said. "I saw him in a catalog several years ago. I'm glad we could finally afford to buy him."

"It was really nice of someone to donate that money to the library," said Sydney. "The Children's Area looks so much nicer!"

Mrs. Mackenzie smiled. "The library is very lucky to have people who care about it. And I'm extra lucky because I have my Book Bunch to help me!"

"Then we'd better start helping," Abby said. "Show us the books we need to move."

"They're right around the corner here," said Mrs. Mackenzie.

Abby walked around the corner and stopped in amazement. One whole wall was covered in gray stones. There was an arched window painted high on the wall. A beautiful gold and red tapestry hung below it.

"Mrs. Mackenzie!" Abby cried. "When did you paint all this?"

Mrs. Mackenzie grinned. "I thought your idea was so wonderful, I couldn't wait to start. I began Monday night after you left. Then, I painted all day yesterday and stayed late last night to finish this wall."

Dakota spun around looking at everything. "This is awesome!" he said. "We have the best library ever!"

The Contest

Abby stood in the hall outside her classroom on Friday morning. She fingered the edge of her gold scarf. She smoothed the folds of her purple dress for the fourth time. *Tap, tap, tap!* Her foot tapped the floor nervously.

Zachary and Dakota poked at each other with their swords and joked with the other boys. Abby was much too worried to joke.

Mr. Kim and Principal Madison were already sitting in their classroom. The contest was about to begin. Mr. Kim was so nice. He even allowed Miss Pringle's class to go first.

One by one Miss Pringle's class filed down the hall. One girl was dressed like a princess. A boy wore red robes and a crown made out of foil. Another boy wore a long, brown robe with a cross around his neck.

Sydney slipped her hand into Abby's. "Don't worry," she whispered. "We're still going to win."

Then, they heard something rolling down the hall. Everyone turned to see what was coming. Dakota and Zachary stopped banging their swords together. They stood motionless staring up the hallway.

"What is it?" Abby asked. It was hard to see through all the other kids.

Dakota gasped and closed his eyes. He turned to face her. "It's a castle," he said with a groan. "They've got a castle on a wagon!"

Abby stood on tiptoe but she still couldn't see. The wagon's wheels squeaked as it rolled down the quiet hall.

"What kind of castle?" Sydney whispered.

"It's a cake," Zachary hissed. "It's a big, huge cake with tons of icing and flags. It's totally awesome."

"Oh no," Sydney said faintly.

Miss Pringle's class wheeled the castle cake closer. The castle's flags waved gently. Its ice cream cone towers

shimmered. Its gumdrop bridge glistened with sugar as it crossed a blue icing moat.

Sydney collapsed against Abby. "We're finished," she whispered. "We'll never win now."

Abby couldn't take her eyes off the cake. It was perfect! It must have taken hours of work. She watched unhappily as the students rolled the glorious creation into her classroom. Principal Madison gasped and clapped in surprise.

"They checked out all those library books on purpose!" Dakota snarled.

Abby sighed. "Mrs. Mackenzie found books for us, too," she reminded him.

"But none of us thought of making a cake!" Sydney said in disgust. "I'll bet they'll even offer to share it with us! That will just win them more points with Principal Madison."

Zachary smacked his sword into the wall. "We did all this work for nothing!"

"We had fun!" Abby said. "Remember that day my dad made your swords? We had a good time."

"But we are going to lose!" Sydney said, jerking at the ribbons on her dress.

"All of us have great costumes," Abby said hopefully. "Maybe Principal Madison doesn't like cake."

Zachary made a face. "Who doesn't like cake?" he asked.

"I don't know," said Abby. "Maybe he's on a diet."

"We should be so lucky," Dakota snapped. "We're doomed!"

Abby stood up straight. She remembered what Gram had told her. "Just do your best," she said. "Mr. Kim must feel awful, too. Let's make him proud!"

The Losers

No one wanted to go to the lunchroom after the contest. Miss Pringle's class was still clapping and cheering. Principal Madison had declared them the winners. They shared their castle cake with the entire elementary school at lunch. Abby and Sydney didn't eat any even though it was chocolate.

Friday afternoon dragged. Bits and pieces from the contest lay in scattered heaps around Mr. Kim's room. No one bothered to pick them up. Mr. Kim kept telling everyone what a good job they had done. But it didn't make anyone feel any better.

Finally it was time to go home. Abby and Sydney dodged five boys from Miss Pringle's class. They were singing "We are the champions!" as they ran down the hall.

Abby and Sydney hurried past them. They went out through the doors and into the cold air.

Sydney crossed her arms over her chest and made a face. "I wish they would quit gloating!" she said.

"I just wish we had something to gloat about," said Abby.

Sydney's mom waved to them from her car.

"Now I have to tell my mom about the contest," Sydney said unhappily. "I'd better go. I'll see you tomorrow at the library."

"Bye," said Abby. Today was supposed to be such a happy day. Now everything was ruined. Her feet dragged as she walked down the steps.

Gram was waiting by the piles of snow at the bottom.

Abby's princess hat dangled from her hand. She didn't even look up at Gram's face. "We lost," she said miserably.

Gram put her arm around Abby. "That's all right," she said. "I'm sure Miss Pringle's class is celebrating."

Abby nodded. "They sure are! They celebrated all afternoon. Every time they saw one of us, they shouted that they were the winners."

Gram laughed. "I imagine that Dakota and Zachary would have done the same thing if they had won."

"Maybe," Abby said. She thought Dakota would have been incredibly excited if they had won. He would have been great at gloating!

"Everybody likes to win," Gram said. "It's never fun to lose."

"I'll say," Abby said, kicking at a clump of snow.

"I'd be happy to order pizza for supper," Gram offered.

"That's okay," Abby said. "It's not the same."

"What grade did you get for your project?" Gram asked as they walked home.

Abby glanced up. "I got an A," she said.

Gram squeezed her shoulder. "Good for you!"

"Sydney got an A, too," Abby told her. "Thank you for making our dresses. Miss Pringle's class only had one princess. Her dress wasn't nearly as pretty as ours were."

"I was over at the library this morning," Gram said. "Mrs. Mackenzie painted the wall by the window. It looks really nice. She said to tell you that she needs two princesses to pose for her tomorrow."

Abby smiled. "Really?" she said. "It will be fun to wear my dress again. I'll call Sydney as soon as I get home."

"You'd better call Zachary and Dakota, too," Gram said. "Tell them to bring their swords and shields. Mrs. Mackenzie wants to paint them, too."

Abby put her princess hat on her head. The scarf glittered and swirled in the wind. "I guess we're still working on a project!" she said. "The Book Bunch is going to be painted on our library's wall! I can hardly wait until Miss Pringle's class sees it!"

Out to Lunch

Mrs. Mackenzie asked the Book Bunch to go out to lunch on a snowy Saturday. Gram drove Abby and Sydney to the library. They climbed out of the car and held their long dresses up out of the snowdrifts.

"Don't forget your hats," Gram said.

"We won't," Abby said. She grabbed her hat and Sydney's. Abby fitted hers onto her head. Snowflakes drifted down. They sparkled like diamonds in Abby's gold scarf.

"Have a good time!" Gram said waving.

"We will!" called Abby. "Thank you!" She handed Sydney her hat.

"Why do you think Mrs. Mackenzie asked us to wear our medieval dresses to lunch?" Sydney asked.

"My dad thinks she wants to take a picture," Abby said, opening the library door.

The children's area looked awesome after two weeks of work! Mrs. Mackenzie had finished the murals. The Book Bunch had worked very hard to move books into the new bookcases.

Abby's dad had made a wooden arch. It covered the bookcases at the entrance. Mrs. Mackenzie had painted it to look like stones. She had even painted little spiders and a mouse peeking out of the wall. Gram sewed red flags with gold tassels to hang from the top.

Abby spun around. "I just love this!" she said. "It's like being inside a fairy tale!"

"Look out," said Sydney. "Here come the ogres!"

Abby turned around. Zachary and Dakota walked in with their swords and shields. Abby grinned. "They're not ogres! They're the knights of the lunch table!"

Dakota rolled his eyes. "Where are we going to lunch, anyway?" he asked. "I'm going to feel pretty silly going into Pizza Jack's like this!"

"It's still a secret," Abby said. "Mrs. Mackenzie won't tell anyone."

"Where is Mrs. Mackenzie?" Sydney asked.

Just then Mrs. Mackenzie appeared. She was dressed in a long, black skirt with a white blouse. She had a black vest that laced up the front. A long plaid scarf was draped over her shoulder.

"Mrs. Mackenzie!" Abby said. "You look as though you stepped right out of one of your books!"

"Well, you are all dressed up to go to lunch," said Mrs. Mackenzie. "I thought I would dress up, too!"

"You look beautiful," said Sydney.

Mrs. Mackenzie bowed. "Thank you very much!" she said. "First, we need to pose for a picture. Come over here by your portraits."

Abby smiled every time she saw that mural. It was so cool to see her own face looking back at her from the wall. The Book Bunch was right there for everyone to see!

Abby was surprised to see a newspaper reporter waiting for them with his camera. "Is everyone here?" he asked Mrs. Mackenzie.

"Yes!" said Mrs. Mackenzie. She turned to the Book Bunch and smiled. "The newspaper is doing a story on the new Children's Area. They wanted a picture of the kids who helped me do the work."

Zachary's mouth dropped open. "Really?" he said.

"Yes, really," said the reporter. "It's good publicity! Why don't all of you stand right here in front of the mural?"

So the Book Bunch stood with Mrs. Mackenzie. Dakota and Zachary held up their swords and tried to look fierce.

Abby and Sydney just smiled when he took the picture.

"This will be in Sunday's paper," said the reporter. "We always try to include good news on the weekends. Tell your parents so they can buy an extra copy!"

"My dad will buy 40 million copies!" said Zachary. "This is awesome!"

Dakota waved his sword. "Yeah, awesome!" he said.

"Are you ready to go to lunch?" asked Mrs. Mackenzie.

"Yes!" they all cheered.

The Castle

The Book Bunch piled into Mrs. Mackenzie's little blue car. Sydney sat with the boys in the back. Abby sat up front.

Abby giggled. She saw glitter on the floor of the car. There was more on the dashboard. Even the steering wheel sparkled!

Mrs. Mackenzie drove out of Evergreen. The road wound around snowy hills and fields. They crossed a bridge and headed toward a golf course.

"Are we almost there?" asked Zachary.

"Almost," said Mrs. Mackenzie. She made a right turn into a driveway with high stone walls. A big sign read "Windsor."

Zachary and Dakota hung over Abby's seat so they could see.

Suddenly, Dakota pounded on the seat. "I know where we're going!" he yelled in Abby's ear. "This place looks just like . . ."

"A castle," whispered Abby. There in front of them was an enormous stone building. Flags flew from the towers. A bridge crossed a frozen stream that circled the front. Snow frosted the walls just like icing.

"It looks like Miss Pringle's cake!" said Sydney.

"It's a restaurant," said Mrs. Mackenzie as she parked the car. "Wait until you see the inside!"

The Book Bunch jumped out and climbed the steps. The huge double doors were heavy and thick. The doorknobs were shaped like dragons!

Zachary ran his hand over the dragon's head. "Cool," he said.

They walked inside. Candles flickered to light their way. Suits of armor stood on display in the hall. A tapestry with a beautiful unicorn hung on the wall.

Abby was so glad that she was wearing her medieval dress. She felt just like a real princess!

The waiters and waitresses were dressed in medieval costumes, too! Their table was by a huge fireplace. The logs crackled and snapped. The chairs looked like thrones! Abby sat between Mrs. Mackenzie and Sydney.

"This is so nice," Abby said. "Thank you!"

Mrs. Mackenzie smiled. "Thank you!" she said. "I appreciate everything

that the Book Bunch does to help me. This is just a special treat."

"I'm glad someone gave that money to the library!" said Dakota. "Or we would never have gotten to come here."

"I'm glad too," said Mrs. Mackenzie.

A waitress brought a basket of bread. The boys each grabbed a breadstick.

"We're starving," said Zachary.

Everyone laughed.

Abby leaned closer to Mrs. Mackenzie. "Will you ever tell us who gave the money to the library?" she asked.

Mrs. Mackenzie shook her head. "I can't tell you," she said. "The person who made the donation to the library asked me not to. He wants to remain anonymous."

"I want to be anonymous," Dakota said.

Sydney laughed. "You can't be anonymous," she said. "Everyone knows who you are!"

"But you could do something nice for someone without telling them who did it," Mrs. Mackenzie replied. "Then you would be an anonymous giver."

Dakota thought for a minute. "Maybe I'll do that," he finally said. "Wait and see!"

Zachary opened his menu. "Wow!" he shouted. "They have Dragon Burgers here!"

"And Princess Pie," Sydney said. "It's chocolate and raspberry! It sounds yummy!"

Dakota laid his sword on the table and leaned back in his chair. "This is way better than a pizza party!"

Zachary stuck a breadstick in his mouth. "Oh, yeah!" he said with a grin.

Give Anonymously

Everyone likes to be thanked for doing something special. But sometimes it is fun to do something anonymously! It makes you feel good! Here are some ways that you can make someone else's day a little brighter. Be sure to leave them guessing as to who did something nice for them!

• Ask your parents to help you bake cookies for a neighbor. Leave them on the neighbor's porch or by the door.

• Vacuum the carpet or wash the dishes to surprise your parents!

• Make a card and send it to someone special.

• Return a stray grocery cart to the cart return.

• Pick up toys and put them away at your library.

• Rake leaves for a neighbor.

- Give outgrown toys or clothes to a homeless shelter.

- Make a happy face and put it on your teacher's desk.

- Pick up trash in the park.

- Visit the elderly in a nursing home near you.

- Make cards and ask your parents to send them to soldiers in the military. There are several places that will forward your message on to our heroes including

  http://www.amillionthanks.org.

- See how many other ways you can think of to be an anonymous giver!